STOP BULLYING BOBBY!
Helping Children Cope with Teasing and Bullying

Dana Smith-Mansell

Illustrations by
Suzanne Riggio

New Horizon Press
Far Hills, New Jersey

Dedicated to "Bobby," who showed true strength of spirit
in the face of adversity, and for Linda, wherever you may be —
thank you for befriending a little boy so long ago.

In loving memory of Helen E. Smith, a believer in dreams.

To encourage all children to develop an awareness,
caring, understanding and tolerance for others.

Copyright © 2004 by Dana Smith-Mansell

Requests for permission should be addressed to:
New Horizon Press
P.O. Box 669
Far Hills, NJ 07931

Smith-Mansell, Dana:
    Stop Bullying Bobby!: Helping Children Cope with Teasing and Bullying

Cover Design: Norma Ehrler Rahn
Interior Design: Bradley Ross

Library of Congress Control Number: 2004108078
ISBN-13: 978-0-88282-253-2

SMALL HORIZONS
A Division of New Horizon Press

16   15   14   13   12   2   3   4   5   6

Printed in the U.S.A.

My name is Robin. I live in a quiet neighborhood with shade trees and lots of families who have children. There is always someone with whom to play in our yards or at the playground.

One day I was flying a kite with my friends Gail and Scott when we saw a boy running down our street.

Then we heard other kids yelling "fraidy cat," "dumbo" and "baby." Their feet pounded on the sidewalk as they ran after the little boy. As he got closer to us, I said to my friends, "I know him. He is in my class. His name is Bobby Jones. He and his mother are new to the neighborhood."

Bobby was seven, just like me, but he was very short, shorter than the kindergarten kids. He had brown hair and thick glasses. Bobby always wore button down shirts and dress pants instead of jeans and t-shirts like the other boys.

"Bobby!" I called. "Why are the kids trying to catch you?" He didn't answer me. His face was red. The bigger children were catching up to him and were still shouting. I felt upset, but I didn't know how to stop them.

At the dinner table that night I told my parents, "I saw Bobby from down the street being chased by some kids."

My dad looked thoughtful. "Robin, could they have been playing a game?"

"I don't think so," I replied. "The kids were calling him bad names and Bobby seemed scared."

"Well, the next time you see Bobby, why don't you ask him what was happening," my dad said. "If it was not a game and the children are making fun of Bobby, we'll talk to his mother and see what we all can do."

"Okay, Dad," I said.

"Good. We'll talk when you get home from school," Dad said. "Don't worry. We'll find ways to help Bobby."

We finished our dinner and I did some homework with Mommy. Then I got into my bed. Daddy and Mommy took turns reading me a story. When they finished, they kissed me and tiptoed out of my room. For a long time I couldn't sleep. I lay there thinking of how sad Bobby looked.

Bobby wasn't at the bus stop the next morning. The bus left without him and came to a stop in front of the school right on time.

As I was getting off the bus, some kids behind me began pushing and shoving. I moved out of their way, as I didn't want to fall. "Why are you all in such a big hurry?" I asked. They didn't answer me and kept pushing their way to the door. I looked out the window to see why they were in such a big rush. Bobby was coming down the street. The kids began chasing and teasing him as soon as they got off the bus. Some, like Daniel, Carol and James, were a lot bigger and ran faster than Bobby. They caught up with him and made a circle around him.

I yelled, "Stop! Leave him alone!"

They didn't listen to me. Bobby was so little I had to stand on my tiptoes to see him. When I did, I could see Carol pulling Bobby's hair. James made fun of him, pointing to Bobby's clothes. More kids made a circle around him. I saw that he was shaking, but he didn't try to run away. He just sadly looked from one kid to the other. Finally, the teacher called us inside. The kids disappeared. Bobby just stood there.

At recess, the bigger kids teased Bobby again. One boy pushed him off the swing set. Another one shouted, "Baby, baby, stick your head in gravy" at him.

I tried to find a teacher. My parents always told me that if I saw something bad happen, I should find an adult. By the time I found Ms. Wells, though, the kids who had been picking on Bobby had gone back inside the building.

That afternoon Bobby looked miserable. I asked, "Why do those kids pick on you all the time?"

He spoke very softly and shook his head, "I don't know."

"Well, you should tell our teacher and your parents," I said, stomping my foot.

"It's okay. It really doesn't bother me," he said. Then his face grew red and he turned away from me.

"Bobby, I know the things they say hurt you," I said.

He gave a little sigh. We talked some more and Bobby blurted out, "I cry myself to sleep every night because of what the kids do to me."

I shook my head. "I can't believe that those kids are so mean to you."

Tears ran down his cheeks. It was the first time I had seen Bobby cry. When I got home, I told my parents what had happened and what Bobby had said.

"I will speak to Bobby's mother," my mother told me.

I still felt upset the next morning, so my mother decided to walk me to the bus stop. On our way there, I saw Bobby walking very fast down the street.

I called to him, "Hey, Bobby, are you going to school today?"

"Yes," he replied, "and I don't want to be late!"

Before Mom and I could cross the street, Bobby had passed the bus stop.

I called to him again, "Hey, Bobby, aren't you going to wait for the school bus?"

"Nope. I am going to walk to school," he replied gloomily. Suddenly, some other kids came around the corner and started running after Bobby. They began to push and throw wads of paper at him. He raced across the street and stood shaking beside my mother and me.

"I hate the bus!" he said angrily. Then he lowered his head and said softly, "The kids just won't leave me alone."

As Bobby turned to leave, my mother reached out her hand to stop him.

"Bobby? I've decided to drive Robin to school this morning. Why don't you come with us? I work at the school, you know."

Bobby smiled as he looked up. "Really? Do you mean it?"

I smiled back and said, "We sure do! Come on!"

"We'll walk over and get permission from your mom," my mother said. "I'm sure it will be okay. No sense in walking all that way when you can ride with us."

"Thanks," said Bobby, grinning from ear to ear. "That would be great!"

Bobby's mom was in the front hall getting ready to go to work when we got to the house.

"June," my mother said, "I am going to drive Robin to school and if it's all right with you, I'll take Bobby, too. Some of the bigger kids were bullying him at the bus stop."

"Bobby, why didn't you tell me?" his mother asked.

Bobby shook his head. "You work so hard to support us since Dad died. I didn't want to make you cry again," he replied.

"Bobby, you can always tell me about anything that's bothering you. Teasing and taunting are just plain wrong. I have to go to work now, but tonight we'll talk about how we can make things better at school."

"I work in the principal's office," my mom said. "If it's all right with you, I will talk to Bobby and Robin's teacher today about the other kids bullying him."

When we got to school, my mom took Bobby and me to our classroom.

After Mommy and Ms. Wells talked, Ms. Wells called Bobby and me over to her desk. "Please stay after class today. We'll talk about how the boys and girls can understand and get to know Bobby better so they won't bully or tease him anymore."

At three, right after class was over for the day, Bobby, Ms. Wells and I had our talk while we ate cookies in the teacher's lounge. It was very cool. I told Ms. Wells how I had seen the kids being mean to Bobby over and over again.

"I wish you had told me, Bobby," Ms. Wells said.

"I don't like to be a tattletale," Bobby said, "but it feels so bad to be made fun of all the time."

"You have been a brave boy," Ms. Wells told Bobby, sighing and patting him on the back. "Bobby, I am so sorry. When things like this happen, it is better to tell an adult who can help. Promise me from now on you will tell me or your mom or someone else you trust when bad things happen."

"I will," Bobby said.

"Good. Tomorrow, a very nice man named Doctor Todd will be coming to class and presenting a puppet play in which you two and all the other kids will have parts."

Bobby looked confused. "We have not practiced. How can we be in a play?"

"That is a surprise," Ms. Wells said with a smile. "You will see."

Suddenly we saw Bobby's mother come into the room.

"Here is another surprise," said Ms. Wells. "Thank you for coming, Mrs. Jones." She turned to me and said, "I have called your mother, Robin, and she says it is okay for you to ride home with Mrs. Jones."

Mrs. Jones hugged Bobby and then me saying, "Robin, thank you for being Bobby's friend. Your mother and I are going to the parents' meeting on Friday night. We'll be making new rules to stop bullying and teasing on school grounds so all kids will feel safer."

I felt happy about that.

That night at dinner, I told my mom and dad about the plan Ms. Wells, Bobby and I had made. I told them about the play we were going to be in and how Bobby's mom was going to help. My mom and dad smiled.

Dad said, "Bobby is very lucky to have a friend like you! Now he knows some kids really do care about him!"

That made me feel good inside. "Bobby is a very nice boy," I said. "When kids get to know him, they will see that!"

I made a promise to myself that I would always be Bobby's friend and show everybody what a good friend he was too!

Bobby's mom took us to school the next morning. When we walked into our classroom, Bobby and I were amazed. All of the tables had been arranged in a semicircle. On each one was a silver paper bag. In front of Ms. Wells's desk was a tall screen. A lovely scene of trees, flowers and a tiny stone house had been painted on it. In the middle was a big square opening, like a stage.

"Please be seated," called Ms. Wells. A man sat next to her. As soon as we all sat down, the man stood up and walked behind the screen. Suddenly, a tall puppet with green skin, dressed in a long blue gown and a pointed hat, appeared on the stage.

"Good morning, boys and girls," said the puppet in a deep voice. "I am Monsieur Todd, the wizard. Welcome to my magic land and to your new selves. Inside the bags on your tables you will find your new name and the puppet person you will be for our game. In a few minutes, you will come up to the stage with your puppet. I will ask you to tell the class all about your puppet. No matter what your puppet looks like, tell the class why it can be a good thing. Now, everyone stand up. First, I will shake my magic wand. Everyone blink three times. Now, ready, get set, open your silver bags!"

There were squeals, laughter and mumbles as the kids looked over their puppets. My puppet had bright red hair and freckles. Her name was Susie. Bobby was sitting next to me. He held his puppet up for me to see. I giggled. Bobby's puppet was much taller than mine. His name was Kevin. Kevin looked like a giant next to Susie.

"Has everyone had a chance to get to know their puppets?" Ms. Wells asked.

"Yes, Ms. Wells," we responded.

"I am going to call you up one at a time to introduce your puppet to the class. Robin, please start."

I walked up to the front of the classroom, putting my puppet, Susie, through the opening in the curtain.

"My name is Susie. I am in second grade. I like reading and horseback riding. Red hair and freckles are really cool. Very few people have red hair, so I stick out in a crowd. It's fun to hear people say that I have pretty hair."

At first, I felt funny being a puppet talking to my class. I felt like I could say whatever I wanted, because I was hidden behind the screen. I liked being Susie for a little while. It was fun to be someone who looks different and does different things. Afterward, though, I was glad to be my real self again.

"Thank you, Robin," Ms. Wells said when I was finished. "Who will be next?"

Daniel was next. "Hi, my name is Nick. I'm eight years old and I weigh a lot. I might look too big to be good at riding a bike, but I ride really fast."

Next, Jen walked up to the stage. Jen's puppet was named Caty and was very tiny. I had to stand up to see her. "I'm Caty and I'm eight. People think I'm really small, but that's good, because I want to be a gymnast and go to the Olympics."

Carol said her puppet, Emily, had braces. "Braces are so cool," Emily said. "You can get cool colored rubber bands to put on them for holidays or just for fun."

The last one to be called up to the stage was Bobby. I knew Bobby felt shy, because so many kids had teased him, but Bobby always acted bravely. He walked right behind the screen and made his puppet wave to the classroom.

"Um…hi. My name is Kevin. I am really tall. Some people make fun of me and call me a giant. I'm not a giant. In fact, being tall is really cool. You can see farther than anyone else. You can reach stuff on shelves that no one else can. Kids my age have to look up to see me. That is really cool, too."

Bobby made Kevin do some funny dance moves. The whole class started laughing. The more the class laughed, the more Bobby made Kevin dance. At the end, he made Kevin bow.

We all started clapping as Bobby walked to his seat. He was blushing, but I could see a smile on his face.

Then Doctor Todd walked back behind the screen and his puppet, the wizard, popped up on the stage.

"That was great, everyone," the wizard said. "You all did very well at becoming someone else for a while. Now let's talk about what we learned from our puppets."

Then Doctor Todd stepped out from behind the screen and stood in front of the class. He put his puppet on the desk and said, "Carol, tell me about your puppet."

"Emily has braces," Carol said.

"Would you make fun of Emily?"

"No. Emily is cool."

"Would you make fun of someone else who has braces?"

"No, there's nothing wrong with having braces. My sister has braces."

"Daniel, your puppet was heavy, but what could he do?" Doctor Todd asked.

"He could ride his bike fast."

"That's right," Doctor Todd said, nodding. "So what did we learn from everyone's puppets?"

The class was silent. No one seemed to know the answer. Then Bobby raised his hand.

"Everyone is different and that is a good thing, not a bad thing."

"That's right, Bobby. Every puppet is different just like every person is different. Just because someone has braces or is tiny or tall or heavy or thin does not mean we should make fun of him or her. We are all different and we are all special in our own ways. Can I count on all of you to be nice to other kids, as nice as you would like them to be to you?"

"Yes!" the class called back.

"Good! Then we've found out something very important today." Doctor Todd exclaimed.

After school, Bobby and I were headed to the bus to go home. Daniel walked up to us. I was worried that he would start picking on Bobby again. "Hey, Bobby," Daniel said, "that dance you had your puppet do was really neat. Maybe one day you can show me how to do it."

"I'll be happy to do that," Bobby said.

"I'm sorry I was mean to you the other day."

"Thanks," Bobby said. "It's all right." He reached out to shake Daniel's hand and Daniel shook Bobby's. We got on the bus and Bobby smiled all the way home.

WAYS CHILDREN CAN COPE WITH BULLYING

1. Tell an adult when someone is bullying you or your friends.

2. Don't be afraid to tell a bully to leave you alone.

3. Talk to your parents or another adult about how you feel.

4. Be able to laugh at yourself.

5. Avoid places and situations where bullying might happen.

6. Make friends with other kids.

7. Don't let bullies see that their teasing bothers you.

8. Don't blame yourself for being bullied. It's not your fault.

9. Believe in yourself.

10. Treat others as you want them to treat you.

WAYS PARENTS, TEACHERS AND OTHER ADULTS CAN HELP CHILDREN WHO ARE BEING BULLIED

1. Be positive and find out all you can about what's happening from the child's perspective.

2. Be supportive and listen closely to what the child says and how he or she feels.

3. Explain to the child what "bullying" behavior is dangerous.

4. Empower victims by supplying consequences for bullies.

5. Become as educated as possible about bullying and what can be done. See resources.

6. Work with the school and other parents to establish clear rules about bullying and teasing in order to prevent such behaviors.

7. Teach children to avoid bullies. If necessary, speak to a teacher or bus driver about changing the child's seat or place in the class-room in order to prevent more occurrences of teasing.

8. Inform children how important it is to tell a teacher or other school authority about instances of dangerous bullying.

9. Go over possible scenarios with children to help them act out positive ways to handle bad situations.

10. Encourage children to make other friends. Bullies are less likely to target children in a group.

11. Give children a feeling of control by explaining their options and encouraging them to think about how to change their situations.

WAYS TO HELP BULLIES CHANGE

1. Label teasing that is mean harmful so there is no doubt that the behavior is negative.

2. Work with the child on emphasizing less hurtful behaviors so the youngster will feel good about him or herself.

3. Reinforce those behaviors which are positive.

4. Be sure there are consequences for bullying.

5. Give the child helpful roles at home and in school.

6. Teach the child to give compliments not taunts and then reinforce this behavior.

7. Give the child "time outs" to reflect on bad behavior.

8. Intervene when necessary to stop cruelty.

9. Teach the child to gain praise by helping others.

10. If bullying becomes physical cruelty, tell the child about possible future legal punishment.

11. Talk individually to the child who is bullying. Perhaps there also are problems with which he or she needs help.

PLACES TO CALL FOR HELP OR ADVICE:

National Anti-Bullying Hotline: (877) 443-9943

Kids Help Phone: (800) 688-6868

WeTip Anonymous Crime Reporting Hotline: (855) 86-BULLY

National Suicide Prevention Lifeline: (800) 273-TALK

WEB SITES TO VISIT FOR HELPFUL ADVICE

Bullying.org: *www.bullying.org*

StopBullying.gov: *www.stopbullying.gov*

Bullying in Schools and what to do about it: *www.kenrigby.net*

Stop Bullying Now: *www.stopbullyingnow.com*

Helping Kids Deal with Bullies:
www.kidshealth.org/parent/emotions/behavior/bullies.html

Let's Talk About Bullying: *www.cbe.ab.ca/new/bullying.asp*

American Academy of Child and Adolescent Psychiatry:
www.aacap.org/publications/factsfam/80.htm

Focus Adolescent Services: *www.focusas.com/Bullying.html*

National Youth Violence Prevention Resource Center:
www.safeyouth.gov/Resources/Pages/Resources.aspx

Bullystoppers.com: *www.bullystoppers.com*